Ribaldry: Sex, Porn and Off-Color Poems

Daniel F.X. Peterson

DEDICATION

I dedicate this little book to Anacreon, Catullus, Horace, Ovid, Petronius, Sappho and Virgil— and also to Julina, who inspired it.

—DFXP 8/31/24

Table of Contents

The Adventure

I am a sex adventure
    man,
A regular explorer;
I give and take what
    thrills I can
With ev'ry cute him or
    her.

I stop at nothing safe
    and clean;
Bodies are my delight.
My partners all know
    what I mean,
When I say I do it right.

Variety that would
    perplex,
Fantastic carnal
    benders,
Amazing and exotic
    sex
With people of all
    genders.

To guard against dis-
    eases foul,
Or cure erectile
    flops,

The pharma bus' ness
     saves the day;
The meds they have are
     tops.

So please view my
     activities
With a fair, observant
     eye;
Condemn not my
     proclivities
If you have to wonder
     why.

Just know that I am
     stable,
And safe and in good
     health,
And think me always
     able
To enjoy my fleshly
     wealth.

There's seldom been an
     easier
Agenda to get done;
It couldn't be much
     sleazier
And still be this much fun!

—DFXP 7/4/23

Always Wash *

I love to jerk and cum
With something in my
   bum,
While dildos are fun,
When I'm on the run,
I often just use my
   thumb;

And though it gets smelly
   I hope
You won't think that I'm
   such a dope:
I finish my jerk
And go back to work
After some water and
   soap.

(If male anal/rectal
penetration and stimu-
lation are morally and
religiously wrong, why
did God give us guys
an extra pleasure organ
in our asses?)

*Anthem of the 'Stinky
Finger Club,' of which

I am a proud member.

—DFXP 9/23/24

All Good

Whatever in life may
    befall,
What will matter most
    after all
Is never the size—
You'll find you will
    prize
Hard penises both
    great and small.

—DFXP 3/14/24

Asshole

Your puckering hole's
    nice and clean,
There's nothing about
    it obscene,
And although I'm
    not young,
It's THE spot for
    my tongue,
And the nicest that
    it's ever been!

—DFXP 2/24/24

Assturbation

We all do things for
	pleasure;
We wank or flick our
	bean;
But the way beyond
	all measure
Is the method that I
	mean:

What's needed is a
	finger,
Or a dildo tried and
	true;
That stinky stuff not
	linger,
Use an enema or
	Two;

Rubber gloves may be
	employed,
And some their condoms
	swear by,
In either case you're
	overjoyed
By the feeling produced
	thereby;

I'm talking about anal
    play,
Insertion in the rectum;
Admirers all of buttholes
    say
They never would
    neglect 'em;

Yes, there's a risk of
    smelly toys,
And some question the
    worth;
But experiencing such
    nether joy's
The greatest rush on
    Earth!

—DFXP 6/30/23

The Beautiful Belly-Button

Flirting with guys was
   her shtick,*
Her beauty and grace
   did the trick,
And by far the best
   feature
Of this ravishing
   creature
Was her stunning (and
   lint-free) pupik.**

—DFXP 1/27/24

* routine or gimmick (Yiddish)
**belly-button (Yiddish)

The Bed-Bound Fart

It sometimes happens
   late at night,
The lights are off, you're
   tucked in tight,

When suddenly you have
   a start,
And realize you need to
   fart,

The blanket's warm, the
   bed is cozy,
You can't get up, you're
   far too dozy,

And though you are a
   lovely lass,
Even beauties must pass
   gas,

You agonize, the point is
   moot,
No compromise, you've
   got to poot,

And so you yield to the
   seduction,
Relief brought by rear-

end eruction,

All will be well, so one
    assumes,
And you believe—
    until the fumes,

You need a plan, you've
    got to think,
But how can you with
    all that stink?

You only hoped and
    sought for peace
From sulphurous
    methane release,

But now it seems you're
    in despair,
And desperately you
    need some air,

To escape from this
    aroma,
You'd even risk a
    hematoma,

But you're never at
    a loss,
So up you jump, the

blanket toss,

To stave off further
indignation,
An open window's
your salvation.

—DFXP 1/17/24

Bi=Half-Queer

I will take a girl to the
  dance,
And with sex there is
  often romance,
But I will not deny
That I'll play with a
  guy,
And enjoy what he's
  got in his pants.

—DFXP 2/28/24

Bi 2

I like smooth and pretty,
   smart and funny,
If that is you, then call
   me, honey;

I don't care what's
   between your legs,
Sushi's fine, or ham
   and eggs.

—DFXP 9/20/24

Bisexual Pride

The lust in us never
    will tire,
But inflame us with
    amorous fire
For the pleasing
    effects
Of hot, shame-free
    sex
With the women and
    men we desire.

HAPPY JUNE IS PRIDE
MONTH!

—DFXP 5/19/24

Bottoms' Anthem

Ass-fucking might well
    pain us,
And taking it up there
    can drain us,
But a dildo sure can
    train us
To enjoy it in the
    anus!

—DFXP 3/5/24

Charming & Witty

You're charming and witty
And all sorts of pretty
Best bod in the city
(especially each titty!)

—DFXP 9/1/24

Cherry Pie

How can I say how much of a turn-on you are for me?
You may think that strange; we rarely fuck.
But fucking has never been the goal
For me.
(Besides, I hate those fucking condoms.)
To have you, nude, between my legs,
Ass-fucking me with a dildo
While you jerk me off slowly, slowly,
Sensually, comfortably, and talk to
Me, converse intelligently, congenially,
Is as good as it gets.
The orgasm at the end is just
Icing on the cake. You are the bomb.
You are this old man's wet dream!

—DFXP 2/27/23

Chicks with Dicks

I'm hard to type, but
   some folks try,
They say I'm gay or
   pan or bi,

The truth is just a bit
   more hazy,
'Cause first of all, I'm
   woman-crazy,

But at the risk of sound-
   ing formal,
I pray that you don't
   call me 'normal,'

I love vagina-ladies,
   sure,
But also ladies more
   obscure,

Those cuties with a
   little more—
A little extra kept in
   store,

So let me tell you,
   here's the skinny:
They've got an 'outie,'

not an 'innie,'

A package down bet-
    ween their legs,
But ribald verse the
    question begs—

For me, a favorite kind
    of chick,
Is the kind who has
    both balls and prick,

Cross-dressers, queens
    and transes fair:
A sisterhood refined and
    rare,

Hot bodies give a
    pleasant shock,
A pretty face with
    ev'ry cock,

You 'straight' guys know
    not what you lack:
Try perfumed pud—you
    won't go back.

—DFXP 1/30/24

I Love Clean Butts

In living cleanly as can be
I've found some new technology

And so I'm very glad to say
It's an easy-use bidet

It runs on water, don't you see?
No need for electricity

And just to tell you what I mean
The damn thing gets you really clean

And you can take my word for it:
I love the hole but hate the shit!

—DFXP 9/7/23

Crazy But Happy

I'm the crazy pan-sexual poly-am
    guy
I like whatever I see
If you're smooth and you're pretty I
    don't ask why
The world is an oyster for me

And talk about cups running over
    my friend
There's a dazzling display on out
    there
Fleshly delights in a world without
    end
A poly guy hasn't a care

If you happen to see an open-
    face man
With a large and a lopsided
    grin,
No need for alarm or an escape
    plan
You just know where poly-guy's
    been!

—DFXP 5/13/23

Credo

I was trying to figure out what I believe in, sexually that is, and this is what I came up with—I think this about sums it up.

MY BELIEFS:

1. The excitement and pleasure of nudity, one's own as well as that of others (as experienced with all five physical senses), the joy of masturbation, the tenderness and exhilaration of partner sex are God's greatest gifts to humanity.
2. I revere the healthy adult nude human body in all of its forms and genders.
3. I express that reverence through solo and mutual masturbation, shared nudity, body contact and affectionate sexual acts, as well as hugs, kisses, snuggling, soothing words and poetry.

—DFXP 12/10/23

CROOT

It's difficult now to
   refute,
And I think that the
   point may be moot—
With fingers and thumb
I'll make myself cum,
And see if my weenie
   goes "CROOT"

—DFXP 9/6/24

Dat Ass

This beautiful big
blonde-haired lass
Shows off callipygian
mass,
And to be very blunt,
As she strokes her
friend's cunt,
She's rightfully proud
of her ass.

—DFXP 10/2/24

Diarrhea

Intestines churning,
And asshole burning
I sit me down to
   squirt

And toilet pound
With splatty sound
No way I can avert

This fateful dump
My guts will pump
Forever now I think

As with a groan
I sit alone
Surrounded by the
   stink.

—DFXP 5/5/24

Dick Duty

Sometimes you know when
    I'm a loner
I get a solitary boner,

It happens when I think
    of asses
And the hard-on seldom
    passes,

Without a little help
    from me,
So that is why I wank,
    you see

It is my duty, I won't
    shirk it,
I'll just grab my
    cock and jerk it!

—DFXP 3/28/24

Dirty-Butt Cutie

This beautiful chubbie's
 my type,
But her rump can become
 a bit ripe—
Sometimes she will
 sit
And have a great
 shit,
But be a bit lax with
 the wipe;

Her lovers note some-
 thing's amiss,
Which bears mentioning,
 and it's this:
Be wary of crap
When she sits on
 your lap,
'Cause her butt leaves
 a little brown kiss.

—DFXP 9/9/24

Dirty Doggerel or,
Talent for Trash

In contemplating subjects
   few are fonder,
And rarely do they cause
   my thoughts to wander
Like the one to me that
   is a spell or hex,
And that dear lady is
   the realm of sex;

It isn't that I'm altogether
   randy,
Or the rhyming that springs
   up is always dandy,
And never would I injure
   or abuse
My reader with the verse
   that I enthuse;

But carnal rumination
   captivates,
And the muse that brings it
   rarely hesitates,
The words pour forth; my
   heart is all a-flutter:
Alas, my "happy place" is in
   the gutter!

—DFXP 6/27/23

The Dirty Panties

Mistress Julina's so
   impressive,
No praise for her can
   be excessive;

Among the ladies she's
   just tops,
Especially when your
   nut she pops;

But up until a recent
   day
I had a slight complaint
   to say.
To let you know the
   gripe I mean:
Her nether regions
   were too clean;

Her pussy and her
   asshole squeaked
With clean but should
   have proudly reeked;

And so it was the worst
   to tell
That her panties had
   no smell;

By which I'm taken
	quite aback:
No pungent aphrodisiac!

But she hit on a
	solution
To create the right
	pollution;

Her panties worn for
	days on end
Were nearly ready
	to offend;

The road to smelly bliss
	was paved,
And so it was the
	day was saved!

I'm not the sort of
	guy you can't please;
I only needed dirty
	panties.

—DFXP 7/6/23

Donald von Poopinpantz

There is a funny
circumstance
Not due to vagueries
of chance,
But rather to the Turd's
romance
With Big Macs and the
fries from France.
The results of this you
ask, perchance?
He's fat and poops
right in his pants,
Which leads to many out-
raged rants
Because they call him
Poopinpantz.

—DFXP 8/5/24

Donald von Poopinpantz II: Stank-ass

Stay far from the orange
turd Trump,
Especially his stanky-
ass rump,
And never suppose
That holding your nose
Will keep you from
smelling his dump 🤢

—DFXP 9/5/24

The Drag Brunch (a short short story)

I had bought tickets to the drag brunch the previous week. This was at the end of a hot July, but the theme was to be very Halloween—the show was entitled "Witchy Woman." I prepared by going to the bank and taking out $100 in the form of twenty $5 bills. I gave little thought to the theme, even forgetting to mention it to the date I asked, my cross-dressing friend Sonja.

Saturday rolled around. I picked up Sonja at her trailer park. She was dressed in pink, as Barbie. Of course then I remembered that the theme was not Barbie and told her. Nevertheless, she was happy to go as Barbie. Just as well. I was in cutoff jean shorts, sandals and an "I Read Banned Books" T -shirt.

I made the trip into Uptown, to the artists' coffee house venue. We were seated at the bar by a pleasant mustachioed young man dressed in a black 'Wicked Witch of the West' costume—high black peaked hat and all. Margaret Hamilton would have been proud. By swiveling my stool, I found that the spot commanded a view of the entire floor and all of the surrounding tables and spectators.

The show began, with the 'mistress of ceremonies' cracking the obligatory joke that "it costs a lot to look this cheap" along with the usual jesting promises of post-show back room sex for a sufficiently large 'contribution'

The semi-intimate setting was perfect: no stage, with the dancing and lip-synching queens circulating to grab the $5s and $10s enthusiastically waved at them.

The costumes were elaborate and authentic, the music fun and loud, the atmosphere raucous, and the queens sexy and congenial—more than happy to pause on their rounds and pose for a quick selfie.

It was a great show—two hours went by as quickly as it took me to go through nineteen of my twenty $5 bills.

Afterwards, I got a photo op with 'Elvira, Mistress of the Dark.' She was big-breasted, black beehive-wigged and beautiful, looking for all the world like the real Cassandra Peterson in makeup and costume. I was enchanted, almost overcome with a feeling of childlike wonder curiously mixed with incipient lust.

The all-too-brief moment ended. Some of the queens had already made their way to a poorly concealed back room they had been using as a changing area—no door, and right next to the unisex bathroom, guaranteeing a steady stream of passing foot traffic and consequently a more or less complete lack of privacy.

Costumes and accessories were coming off—a very large queen was minus her wig and a good deal of her makeup, and she was now a chubby and entirely bald man.

Part of me wanted to stay, to see what my crush 'Elvira' looked like in her more everyday state.

I remembered the words that Sonja used to repeat frequently when we first met: "it's all about maintaining the illusion."

She was right, of course. I spun on my heel, collected her, and walked out into the summer afternoon, hot-asphalt-smelling parking lot, squinting in the bright sunshine—my illusion behind me, safe in the recent past, in the comfortingly-shadowed cafe.

—DFXP 7/29/23

Dream Lady

When my world a trial
   seems,
The means of my rescue?
A lovely lady from my
   dreams;
The lady, dear, is you.

You fill my soul, you fill my
   arms,
Your body is my joy.
The is no equal to your
   charms,
To this your fortune'd boy.

For when I'm with you,
   sweet, I think
I'm luckier than some:
No need have I for drugs
   or drink
Because you make me cum!

—DFXP 5/17/23

Eating Pussy and Rimming

Like penises, although greatly varying from one to the next, most pussies are attractive.

A nice clean and clean-shaven slot like yours, dear lady, with no protruding labia and a cute little button clit is elegant and ladylike.

Yet a BIG bush, extending to and around the asshole and down the inner thighs, bursting from the panties, is also very attractive to me for some reason.

Likewise big hanging labia, and giant, hooded clits looking for all the world like small penises are enticing to me as well. Dainty or outrageous, as long as it's healthy-looking, it's for me

Good pussy has a smell and a taste. The smell is a body smell—at best somewhat acrid and a bit pungent—the natural aroma of vaginal secretions and mucosa, not harmed but rather enhanced by lingering hints of sweat, urine and anus.

Stereotypically, some pussy can smell a bit fishy. A LITTLE fishy smell is fine and some like it—I myself don't mind it.

But be careful: a yeast-infected vagina is quite stinky—and not in a good way!

So much for smell.

The taste varies from woman to woman, but all flavors are good provided again that the woman is healthy. You can best 'savor the flavor' if you can really get her juices flowing—it pays to be patient and have a strong and nimble tongue. For maximum cleanliness the pussy-eater should have just brushed his or her teeth and used mouthwash. Adding clean saliva to freely flowing lady juice optimizes the experience. Good slurping!

Most pussy tastes slightly sour and acidic, with a delightful tanginess to it.

One woman tasted vinegary to me, but she may have just douched. And sometimes pussy can also taste a little fishy. As with the smell, a little is fine, but a lot is a problem.

If I can find a comfortable position where my mouth is well positioned and I can get a free hand down between my legs to masturbate with, I can edge and lap and enjoy this delicious treat for hours.

Finally: the asshole. Much of the above relates to the asshole as well, and there's nothing like 'snacking on the starfish.' Most anuses are actually very pretty in a puckery sort of way—a look that certainly works for lips (and I've puckered up my lips and planted a few kisses on buttholes in my time)!

Asshole tastes great as long as it's relatively clean, but please, if you haven't bathed since your last poop at least use a wet wipe—I'm not so much into a shitty bunghole.

As far as sex acts go, this one is off the charts, erotically speaking—I'm getting a hard on just typing these words!

Pussy and asshole combined make up a HUGE subject area, so I've no doubt that I have left out a great deal.

My apologies and promise that I will strive to supplement this little piece on occasion, as I am able.

—DFXP 7/15/23

Ending to Excess

I have plumbed the depths of sexual excess.
I have drunk from the cup of perversions.
I have tasted of every depravity.
I have whored; I have queered; I have orgied.
I have been humiliated and humiliated myself in a hundred ways.
And yet it seems that I have barely scratched the surface.
Where do such things end?
How do they end?

—DFXP 9/2/22

Ersatz Girlfriend

A cute redhead I chanced to call
In answer to an ad,
In hopes that something good befall
'Cause I was feeling sad;

For she who was my wedded wife
For over thirty years
Condemned me to a sexless life
Of wanking, porn and tears;

I called and spoke so shyly but
The lady soon agreed,
She said she'd gladly pop my nut
And satisfy my need;

And soon the fated day came 'round
And I was in her presence,
I stood there rapt, without a sound
Basking in her pleasance;

For she was worldly-wise but sweet
And put me at my ease,
Arrangements all were so discrete
It didn't feel like sleaze;

Her body was a wonderland,
She drove me to distraction,
She even made 'Old Willy' stand,

How welcome a reaction!

And each gave each a happy end
Of perfect pulsing joy,
I'm crazy for my temp girlfriend
My brainy, curvy toy!

—DFXP 8/30/23

Exo-Love: A Quickie Alien Porn

"While your appearance does seem strange to me, I understand that among your own kind you are regarded as an exceptional female beauty."

Strlglup's Terran 'English'—while delivered in a curious, halting. nasal alien sing-song accent—was fluent. With a linguistic capability far beyond anything known on Earth, he had mastered the intricacies of the language in mere days.

He—and Strlglup was unquestionably male (or at least his planet's version of male)—regarded the voluptuous nude Earth woman standing before him. He experienced no disgust in the sight, but rather a sexual curiosity—a curiosity which gave way to fascination—and a fascination which gave way to arousal.

He stood, and shed his robes of state. He had a lean, muscular body—something over seven feet in height and bilaterally symmetrical but with some interesting differences—an extra joint in each limb, six long, slender fingers on each hand, and sunken concave chest—all topped by a vertically elongated domed head featuring feathery ears, widely spaced eyes and no nose.

Strlglup's garment lay crumpled at his feet, and his long, slender, twin penises slowly unfurled. While the rest of him was a dull gray color, the penises were purple—but now rapidly changing color to a bright mauve.

Strlglup's face assumed a hideous grimace—his version of a sexy come-hither smile—and he cooed seductively at the Terran female.

Mildred eyed the ridiculously fragile-looking penises with little enthusiasm. She was tired and hungry. She yawned and tried to muster a smile for her soon-to-be sex partner. She wondered if they'd be having any of that alien pizza afterwards—she really liked that stuff.

—DFXP 1/22/24

The Family that Plays Together Stays Together (an Incest/Bisexual Fantasy)

You doggy-style your big
    fat granny,
Pump your jizz right up
    her fanny,

Then you show her what
    you've got,
And put it in her gray-
    haired twat,

But next door there's
    this nice young man,
Who always loves a
    dirty plan,

So when you're done
    with old grandmother,
You and he suck off
    each other,

You bring him off, cum,
    flash a grin,
He wipes your semen
    from his chin,

And then there's some-
    thing you can't miss,

You hide out on your
  lovely sis,

A pretty masturbating
  lass,
You jerk, a finger up
  your ass,

And just before she
  starts to cum,
You switch the finger
  to your thumb,

You moan out loud
  before you think,
With spurting wad
  and finger stink,

But there is no need
  to feel blue,
Your sister made a wet
  mess too,

For last, not least, you
  save 'the bomb,'
Some incest intercourse
  with mom,

And you know it just
  feels right,

'Cause unlike granny,
   mom's so tight,

You eat her pussy 'til
   she cries,
By now you've reached
   your biggest size,

In hot embrace you and
   she clasp,
You put it in and hear
   her gasp,

You thrust, she begs you
   not to stop,
You blow your load and
   then you flop,

She hugs you to her
   breasts with joy—
You're everybody's
   darling boy!

—DFXP 9/22/24

Fap

Dabney was married—for decades. He was still healthy and vigorous. Unfortunately however his long-standing marriage had gradually become sexless (as long-standing marriages often do). That he resorted to porn and frequent masturbation seemed only a matter of course—such was Dabney's sex life for many years, and he had been untroubled by it. What gave him some concern now was the fascination he had developed for gay porn.

More than a fascination, a need. It seemed now that Dabney couldn't even get it up unless immersed in a video of two (or more) guys going at it. Dabney thought of the images all the tits and asses, all the pussies, all of the smooth skin and pretty female faces that had accompanied his self-stimulation down through the years—he almost felt as if he were mourning the loss of an old friend. But carnal necessity was not to be denied: muscular bodies, bearded faces, hairy asses and big, fat ejaculating cocks were now the order of the day.

Dabney stroked hard while staring at screen of his tablet, even as the two male figures he was watching consummated their homosexual lust. Dabney was trembling now, his breathing hard, and he was moaning along with porn actors. The tablet was perched precariously on the edge of the sink at groin level, with Dabney standing before it—furiously stroking the shaft of his erect penis with his right hand while vigorously tugging on his now-swollen ball-sac with his left.
His breath began to come in ragged gasps, as he bent his knees and hunched forward involuntarily, his entire body now committed.

Dabney's right hand was a blur, the strokes now too rapid for the eye to follow.

And then, as the performers on the screen reached orgasm, Dabney did too. Hot semen spurted from his penis, spurt after spurt, rope after rope of the viscous white fluid shooting through space to splatter on the tablet's screen. Dabney thought of the mess but was unable to stop, trembling and still stroking furiously through the magnificent—and extraordinarily voluminous—ejaculation. Dabney shuddered and pumped, partially losing his balance but managing to grab the edge of sink with his left hand. The force of the contractions was beginning to abate now, the hot fluid dropping almost straight down toward the floor rather than shooting out horizontally—but his cock continued to pulse with the contractions. The cum now pooled in a puddle at his feet.

As the last spurts died away, Dabney lost his footing in the slippery sperm-puddle and fell.

He lay on the now-wet tiled floor. He had bumped his forehead on the edge of the sink as he fell—it began to throb. He would have a bruise there for sure, and probably a bump as well.

Cum dripped from the edge of the sink. Dabney—having landed right on the jizz-pool—felt almost as if he were swimming in the now-cold but still viscous reproductive fluid. The iPad looked as if it had been immersed in the white goop, but, remarkably, still seemed to be functioning, the screen frozen between videos.

With a grumble, Dabney sat up, then slowly, painfully got to his feet. He couldn't help seeing himself in the big, ceiling-high mirror. He was messy and a bruise was indeed becoming visible, but he half-grinned as he thought of his superlatively masculine performance. If his wife came in now and saw the dripping sink, the puddle on the floor—both obviously semen—as well as the wet, bruised, decidedly untidy state he was in, he would be embarrassed for sure. But he didn't think that he would be able to hide his pride in his spectacular masturbatory achievement.

Dabney sighed, rubbed his forehead, and grabbed a dirty towel from the hamper to start sopping up all the ejaculate. He got down on the floor and began to mop up the puddle. In that position, naked, on all fours, ass-up, he began to feel very erotic.
His right hand clutched his still slick and rapidly re-hardening dick.
Here we go again, he thought, as he slowly began to stroke....

—DFXP 2/27/24

Farts

A subject very near
 my heart
Is the oft recurring
 fart,

Some are pffts and
 some are BRAAAPs
And some make wet
 and messy craps,

Some are silent, deadly
 too,
Get too close and you
 will rue,

Pretty girls with cutesy
 toots
Will singe your hair
 down to the roots,

Truck drivers at a
 greasy spoon
Will make you want
 to die real soon,

The pooch is often
 man's best friend,
But stay away from

their rear end!

When passing gas
    you must beware,
Please be cautious—
    have a care:

You think a puff is
    all you'll get,
Alas, oh no, you feel
    it's wet!

You shat your pants,
    no, it's not fair—
To Walmart for some
    underwear!

—DFXP 3/16/24

February and May

May wears the visage of
A beauty, hair tousled by fragrant
Breezes, and puckered lips blowing
Carefree kisses.
February is the ass-end of the year;
A damp, messy, dirty posterior,
A rump, a derrière, a butt.
There's puckering going on there
Too, but what issues is not kisses
And is not fragrant.

—DFXP 2/18/23

Friendship Is Hard

I look back o'er the last
two years,
Though it brings me
close to tears,

My mid-life crisis hit me
late,
And rather than resign to
fate,

And a mostly sexless
life,
A quiet nod I gave my
wife

Politely giving her the
slip,
In search of a
relationship,

And so I learned if there's
a hex,
It goes to friendship not
to sex;

Sex is no elusive end
If you have the bucks
to spend,

So many nice folks you
can see
Who sell erotic luxury:
Sex straight and gay
and nice and raunchy
(Even though I'm old
and paunchy)

I had no trouble
finding it,
But soon a sad
idea hit:

While fucking's easy
friendship's not,
Though you may try
to search a lot;

The moral of this
sorry tale:
Real friendship never
goes on sale.

So go you forth and
keep in mind,
A true friend is the
rarest find,

And if you find one
who likes you,

Be sure to give them
their just due,

Don't be a jerk and
ruin it,
Or all your days you'll
feel like SHIT!

—DFXP 10/31/23

Frog Prince

A pretty princess kiss
Will righten what's
    amiss,
But most frogs like
    worms,
And whatever squirms,
So their breath's not
    entirely bliss.

—DFXP 2/23/24

Fuck-Mommy

The banner of sex you
 unfurl,
And put my heart all
 in a whirl,
When spanking my
 bum
And making me
 cum—
You're better than
 any dick-girl!

—DFXP 7/2/24

Funny About Kissing

Sex is odd, but what's
    more funny,
Than giving lots of
    sugar, honey?

I'm the sort of guy
    you see,
Who wants to smooch
    with who's with me,

For comfort and for
    passion too,
I'll want to share my
    lips with you,

Sometimes I ask and
    get a fuck,
Then try to kiss—I'm
    out of luck,

It hurts when I get
    twat or dick,
But not a kiss—as
    if I'm sick

But then I think it's
    'cause, alas,

I just got done
        eating their ass!

—DFXP 2/8/24

Gather Ye Rosebuds, Coy Mistress

Love's not about your
  comfort zone;
True love's jarring to
  the bone;

It's not about security,
A safe love never will
  be free;

It's not for your emotions'
  profit,
Whatever you may get
  out of it;

No, not for any sort of
  gain,
But sweet agony and
  longing pain;

Deluding self to shun
  depression
Is just a masturbation
  session;

You never will love
  to the full,
In semi-comfort that

is dull;

So settle not for
    dregs and dearth,
But LOVE while still
    above the earth.

—DFXP 12/9/23

Greatest Show
on Earth

In thinking of women,
 and mothers,
If I could be granted
 my 'druthers,'
I'd have 'em all
 'bate
'Cause nothing's
 so great
As them wanking
 themselves and
 some others!

—DFXP 9/24/24

Hail to the Queen

The Queen likes to have
    her fun too,
So of partners she has
    quite a few,
She's ready to lick
Every pussy and dick,
And always enjoys a
    good screw;

Her harem of human
    sex toys
Is full of big girls and
    big boys,
And she likes to tease,
And make them say
    please
For the sexual skills
    she employs.

—DFXP 9/22/24

Happiness Is....

It seems right now my
   sex life's set;
I've ceased to cruise the
   internet;

I've transes, whores and
   two CDs,
Quite satisfying if you
   please;

And then there are my
   drag-queen friends,
Providing pleasure at
   both ends;

Plus a great massager
   guy
For men and women—
   it's cool he's bi;

Julina is a dream in
   bed,
Angelic face and hair
   of red;

I seldom lack a sexy
   pal,
Whether it be guy or

gal;

And if I do go on
     'vacation,'
I love my porn and
     masturbation;

And so I'll never be
     depressed,
Because my sex life
     is the best.

—DFXP 7/20/23

Hard Penises

Hard penises never
    know shame,
And every hole looks
    the same,
They're always in
    luck,
Whatever they fuck,
And always so glad
    that they came.

—DFXP 3/23/24

Having Sex vs Making Love

I'll make love to you
If you should want me
   to,
But if you really don't
Of course you know I
   won't.

Sex? No big deal to
   me,
That's something sad
   to see—
To no one else but
   you
Will I make love that's
   true.

—DFXP 10/30/24

Holding Onto
My Treasure

As I drift off to La-La
　　Land
I always clutch my
　　junk in hand,

Cup my balls and
　　grasp my shaft,
Although the world
　　might think me daft,

And think I hold my
　　pubic treasure
Just to get the fleshy
　　pleasure,

But there's a greater
　　reason there,
Because you see I
　　must beware,

It isn't just I like to
　　feel it,
But also I'm afraid
　　they'll steal it!

—DFXP 3/27/24

Horny Mind

When I'm of a horny
   mind
In my arms I seem to
   find
A red-head chick all
   curves and smile,
With whom I'd like to
   spend a while
Just humping her
   behind!*

—DFXP 8/22/24

*And I'd love for you
to hump mine too—
If that is what you'd
like to do!

How Cool R U?

Sex I've had both gay
and straight,
And I can tell you, both
are great;

In one respect queer sex
is tops,
'Cause guys just pull out
all the stops;

They only care for fun
and pleasure,
And cumming is the
greatest treasure;

They do not cling or
jealous wax,
They like to do it then
relax,

And when the suck and
fuck is done,
They slap each other's
ass for fun,

And each then goes his
separate way,
And no one cares where

others stray,

So please don't take it
hard when I
Say I love you like a
guy!

—DFXP 10/6/23

Human Sexuality

Human sexuality is people
Getting naked with each other,
Playing with each others' privates.
It can feel great; it can be a
So nice, so pleasurable, such a
Wonderful bonding experience.
But it can also be not so nice,
Depending on the circumstances,
And it is by no means
The only bonding experience.
Sharing a meal, or a movie, or a
Book or a poem or a conversation
And a cup of coffee or a glass of
Wine can be wonderful bonding
Experiences too, and will probably
Make for more meaningful
Communication, exchange of ideas
At the end of the day.
My vote?
All of the above. ☺
—DFXP 3/24/23

I Broke My Pipes

"I broke my pipes, because they could delight and lead the sturdy herds which way I would, but could not draw the froward girl. For there is no medicine for love, neither meat nor drink nor any charm, but only kissing, and embracing, and lying naked together."

—from "Daphnis and Chloe" by Longus

I Love When
You Wank!

Dear Julina,

I like eating ass
    and pussy too,
The cocks I've
    sucked have
    been a few,

But there's some-
    thing I love even
    more,
A job for hands,
    but not a chore,

I really love to
    beat my meat,
It's my go-to
    special treat,

And helping others
    isn't icky—
Who cares that
    fingers get all
    sticky?

But it don't matter
    if they squirt—

Girls seldom do
    and where's
    the hurt?

They sigh and moan
    in their delight—
The way they shake
    is quite a sight,

Fun with a boy as
    with a girl,
Either way their
    toes will curl!

And when I'm with
    you on a date,
The BEST PART'S
    when you mastur-
    bate!

Kisses, beautiful
redhead bean-
stroker 🖤 🖤 🖤

—DFXP 12/2/23

I Praise Your Pubes

I love the charms
    of my fair lass,
Her lovely tits
    her curvy ass,

But there's one
    thing beyond all these
That always brings
    me to my knees,

It's what she has
    beyond compare:
Exuberance of pubic
    hair!

A luscious nest of
    bushy curls
The pleasure glory
    it unfurls,

The fragrant smell,
    the tangy flavor—
Delights I linger on
    and savor,

And with a pussy-
    beard like this

Her pussy-lips I
    long to kiss.

Forever may this fur-
    flag wave—
She'd break my heart
    if she should shave!

—DFXP 1/13/24

I Remember

I remember intimate moments;
I remember beautiful, lop-sided breasts;
I remember a delicious plump tushie that always sported one or two
little pink pimples;
I remember the wonderful scent of your hair;
I remember another another smell and taste that intoxicated me;
And I remember a beautiful, angelic face, cheerful and happy during
foreplay, and then with that sweetly agonized expression that comes with
orgasm;
I remember.

–DFXP Fall 2021

In Praise of Anus

Derision is never my
   goal
But rather I'm pleased
   to extol
The puckering grace
When it's put in my
   face
Of a beautiful woman's
   asshole.

—DFXP 8/13/24

In Praise of CD
Bottoms

I love CD bottoms—
Most have plump,
Beautiful asses,
Which they will
Present to you so
Erotically framed by
Lace stocking tops
And garter belts—
They will so elegantly
Straddle and sit their
Bottom down onto
Your eager, waiting
Hard-on, cowgirl-style,
Take the head into
Their excited, gaping
Asshole, settle them-
selves down and push
Your stiff manhood
All the way in—glorious
Feeling—then spirited
Fucking begins—they
Ride you like an
English jockey posting
Up and down in the
The saddle—their own
Erection bouncing before
Your eyes, cheerful and

Enthusiastic—you buck your
Hips in rhythm to their
Deep squatting, and both
Of you begin to moan,
Primal, wordless sex duet,
Steadily approaching joy—
Then finally, the inevitable
Explosion—contraction after
Contraction from the balls
And deeper inside, your own
Asshole puckers, relaxes,
Puckers—pulsating to the
Carnal beat, as you pump
The gusher of your hot cum
Into voracious colon, greedy
Rectum—then their own
Explosion and contractions,
Ropes of welcome ejaculate
Arc and splatter your taught
Belly, adding to an ecstasy
Of pleasure—praise to strong
Talented sphincter muscles
—throbbing and throbbing,
Cumming and cumming—
Until finally both finish—
Then they're off you
And collapse in your arms,
Flopping onto your semen-
Spattered stomach, their
Fluid whiteness growing

Cold as it drips down your
Sides onto sweaty sheets
—you hug lazily, now both
Slack—a spell of delicious
Satisfaction and content—
Your own thick white jizz
Begins to dribble out from
Their sore but happy anus.

—DFXP 7/31/23

In Praise of Pan

It seems that I'm the
    type of man
Who is by nature
    mainly Pan,

This god of woodland's
    savage cry
Inspired fear in all
    who'd try

To get to know his lo
    spirit rural
Who's image sports
    on frieze and mural,

A shepherd's patron
    he at first,
With a deep abiding
    thirst

For beauty of the
    human form,
Irregardless of the
    norm

With all young pretties
    he would sleep

(He didn't even stop
  at sheep)

He had a crack at
  Syrinx fair,
But Daphnis mussed
  his pubic hair,

Syrinx was a chick
  you see,
But Daphnis was a
  guy like me,

And so we know
  that nature says
You can be homo
  or be Les

And who you choose
  to hump's your biz,
Enjoy them as you
  squirt or jizz,

The bottom line's
  that it's all good
If you treat lovers
  as you should,

And then you will
  have divine luck

Irregardless* who
you fuck.

—DFXP 3/24/24

(*not really a word)

IN THE END IT'S NOT THE THINGS
YOU DID THAT YOU REGRET–
IT'S THE THINGS YOU DIDN'T DO.

Invictus

You are not bad for me,
But you say that I am bad for you.
I drink.
I do not sleep nights.
My mind wanders.
I'm promiscuous.
I cheat on my wife.
I'm bisexual.
Pansexual.
I want to fuck everyone.
I do not accept my age.
I take Test and Viagra, so that
I can mess around,
And I do, a lot.
I'm that corrections officer
To whose lonely place
You took the train, at night,
And met alone,
And wanked.
You were in danger, and yet
You were safe.
I love you, and that
Confuses you,
Distresses you.
And yet again you are safe.
You love me, but
You look down on me.
I don't mind your contempt

If I can also have your love.
And if I couldn't have your love
I would still take your contempt—
The only thing I couldn't stand,
The thing that would break my heart,
Would be your indifference.
And that I will never have.
I don't wish to brag, but
I am the most romantic man
You will ever meet, and
I love you.
You are still safe.

—DFXP 1/28/23

Insomnia is the
Poet's Friend

Once more you're in
    trouble deep,
It's 3:00 AM and you
    can't sleep,

All kinds of thoughts
    come rushing in,
What you've done and
    where you've been,

Problems faced by our
    whole nation,
The entire global
    situation,

Money, family—lots
    of cares
Just sneak up on
    you unawares,

Could it have been
    something you ate?
Perhaps if you just
    masturbate?

Well, that was fun but
    didn't work,

And now you feel like
    such a jerk,

You try to sleep, but
    thoughts still race,
A hectic look comes
    on your face,

Then swirling thoughts
    start to align,
You start to think things
    may be fine,

You grab a paper scrap
    and pen,
Immerse yourself in
    scribbling then,

Your scrawl and scratch
    for good or ill,
No going back—it's
    seized your will,

The stanzas come both
    thick and fast,
The verses fly from
    first to last,

Then comes the dawn
    and morning light

And it's all down in
    black and white,

A triumph of the
    written word,
Or maybe just a
    rhyming turd,

It matters not, this
    much is true:
Again you've done
    that thing you do,

Now bleary-eyed you
    stretch and yawn,
Blink in the pale light
    of dawn,

Who cares if night's
    now at an end?
Insomnia's the poet's
    friend!

—DFXP 2/11/24

Intersex

I do not mention it
  a lot,
But I think that inter-
  sex is hot,

Not only there's a
  cock to suck,
But you also get
  two holes to fuck,

If body's smooth
  and face is pretty,
Let's just say I won't
  feel shitty,

And if I should die
  while in her arms,
At least I'll have those
  lovely charms,

Let others go and
  fly a kite—
Give me a hot
  hermaphrodite!

—DFXP 2/14/24

Jerkin' My Gherkin

Jerkin' my Gherkin thinkin'
of you,
Grittin' my teeth the whole
time I do,
For while I am squeezing
with fingers and thumb,
I've got to be careful I don't
make it cum!

—DFXP 8/5/24

Jerking to Thoughts

I'm just lying here in
    my bed,
Impure thoughts of you
    in my head,
I play with my dick,
But it don't do the
    trick,
And just makes a big
    mess instead.

—DFXP 2/24/24

Joy of Cum

When wanking please
never make haste,
And don't let it all go
to waste,
Just splooge all that
goo,
Feels so good to do,
Then eat it 'cause you
love the taste.

—DFXP 2/24/24

The Joy of Joy

One need not be a maiden
To be close company
Wherever you have strayed in
You're good enough for me

Be clean and healthy please
And always remain careful
We'll get along with ease
And never need be prayerful

For I like to have my pleasure
Without it I'm forlorn
It's humans' greatest treasure
From the moment we're all born

I enjoy it when alone
Or share it with a crush
Or on the telephone
(The latter makes me blush)

So when you're feeling blue
And life has got you down
Just grab your Sam or Sue
Get busy! Go to town!

DFXP 6/17/23

The King Must Die

The king enjoys
    life in full measure
Surrounded by sensual
    treasure,
As part of his plan
Each nude woman
    and man
Provide sexy bodies
    for pleasure.

And though his life's
    nearing its end,
He does what he can
    to extend
His days full of fucking,
And happy cock-sucking
With every joy-giving
    friend.

—DFXP 9/22/24
(Happy First Day of
Autumn!)

Kiyoko

Such a beauty and talent
    is Kayley
That I can't help but play
    her stuff daily,
But alas how I pine
That she'll never be mine,
So I listen both sadly and
    gayly.

—DFXP 2/4/24

Lazy Guys

Guys like to go
   cruising for chicks,
That's how they get
   their best kicks,
But at times they
   get lazy,
And a little bit
   crazy,
And just hang out
   and play with
   their dicks.

—DFXP 8/13/24

The Legend of Pencil-Dick and Hangy Balls

A legend tells what did befall
Friends 'Pencil-Dick' and 'Hangy
Balls,'

Room-mates and horny dogs were
they,
And usually on Saturday

When female dates were hard to
find,
They'd look with lust at their behind,

And since the ladies just weren't game,
They'd use each other just the same,

And once while they were going strong,
Old Pencil Dick just got too long,

And while his rapier dick he plied,
Poor Hangy Balls went to one
side,

Mis-stepped and on his balls he trod;
The scream he screamed was rather
odd,

Pencil Dick then gave a jump,
His dick broke off in Hangy's
rump

While Hangy clutched his balls
and ran,
Such woes so rarely fall on man

That when they do they are of
note,
And that is why this poem I wrote.

—DFXP 9/15/23

Let Poesy be First, or Petronius on the
Proper Way to Teach Young Men (yes,
it's sexist) to be Poets*

"Whether to Tritonia's famous halls
The Muses lead his steps, or to those walls
That Spartan exiles rear'd or where
The Sirens' song thrill'd the enraptured air
Of all his tasks let Poesy be first,
And Homer's verse the fount to quench his thirst.
Soon will he master deep Socratic lore,
And wield the arms Demosthenes erst bore.
Then to new modes must he in turn be led,
And Grecian wit to Roman accents wed.
Nor in the forum only will he find
Meet occupation for his busy mind;
On books he'll feast, the poet's words of fire,
Heroic tales of war and Tully's patriot ire,
Such be thy studies; then, whate'er the theme,
Pour forth thine eloquence in copious stream."

*From "The Satyricon," translation attributed to
Oscar Wilde

Little Poem

You cheer me up, you
   make me smile,
And when I'm with you,
   all the while

I gaze in rapture in
   your face,
I feel the warmth
   of your embrace;

I love the sex, that much
   is true,
But love it more ' cause
   it's with you;

With you I'll always
   happy be,
And feel the joy you
   bring to me,

And any blues I
   have will pass:
For you I'm just
   tits over ass!

—DFXP 10/12/23

Life Sentences

I am a strange person.

I'm trying not to be egotistical, but it is difficult not to seem egotistical when writing something like this.

I'm not a bad strange, at least I don't feel that I am.

And I don't think that I'm a bad person, but others do.

I have ideas about things—I cannot say that they are all my own.

They're just not the 'normal' ones that we are all supposed to have.

There is the world out there, and there is the world in here. I am ruled less by the world out there than most—but still far more than I would like.

I do not hurt, I do not kill—I love animals and nature and even tolerate my fellow humans. I am also polyamorous and pansexual and that makes me a pervert and a pariah—sins far too grave for the 'good people' to let go by.

To all of those 'good people' I say: Your 'in here' is a steel prison cell, a welded 10 x 10 tank with a metal shelf for a bed and a lidless toilet right in the middle of it. It was constructed for your incarceration long ago and you have willingly spent your life in it.

Perhaps I have never fully escaped mine either, but I try. I try.

FREE YOUR MIND.—DFXP 1/22/23

Love Business

I know a woman plump*
and fair,
With silky skin and
fiery hair;

She gives me comfort
and good sense,
And is well worth the
recompense.

Our bond is a commercial
one,
But with affection, lots
of fun.

I'm fond of her it's true
to say,
But haven't thrown my
heart away.

The barriers are plain
to see,
And she will never fall
for me.

So while no torch I
carry for her,

Within the context I
adore her!

(*pleasantly plump, perfectly plump)

—DFXP 7/5/23

Love-Goo

I'm a mother-fucker,
  true,
And cumming's what
  I love to do:
I give my salami
To pretty Fuck-Mommy,
And she makes it shoot
  my love-goo!

—DFXP 8/22/24

Love or Communism

They say love's patient and
it's kind.
And many say it's also
blind.

True lovers see the common
good,
As everybody knows they
should.

They contribute what they
can afford,
Each one gives and no one
hoards.

But what is this
philosophy?
What is the basis we
can see?

True, Cupid's arrow flies
with sparks,
But in the end we get
Karl Marx.

—DFXP 7/1/23

M Doesn't Fit

I visited M in the afternoon. She is perfectly proportioned and breathtaking naked. But at four feet eleven inches she's so small and things are so close together that it's hard to get at more than one thing at a time. Here's what I mean: if you're firmly in genital-to-genital contact with her, her breasts are about at belly level, and the top of her head is where her breasts should be. The result is that it's really very difficult—and painful— to bend your neck enough to reach her breasts with your mouth. And she's delicate: she complains that a normal amorous embrace "crushes" her.

I need a larger, sturdier, bigger-boned woman. Someone maybe about five feet seven or eight inches—maybe an inch or so less as she got older. Someone built for my hugs, zaftig, with a big ass and plenty of padding to absorb the forces generated by the "snuggle struggle."

I need someone like that, because M doesn't fit.

—DFXP 9/19/22

Male Masturbation

There is a gentle art
    I swear by,
And much improved
    my life is thereby;

The object of this
    adulation?
Of course I'm talking
    masturbation;

Libido and sex
    energy
Cannot be bound and
    must be free;

Thus wanking is a
    useful treat,
For benefits it can't
    be beat:

Your peace of mind it
    helps you keep,
Relieves your stress and
    helps you sleep;

Another help to guys
    you see:
It's very good to treat

ED.

The difficulty faced by
    we men
Is what to do with all
    that semen?

Well, if you can stand
    the test,
It's beneficial to
    ingest:

A nice dose of
    testosterone
Good for muscle and
    for bone,

Mood elevation has a
    hand in:
Oxytocin, prostoglandin,

And just to make you
    feel real keen,
It even gives you
    Dopamine;

So when you're feeling
    lost and lorn,
Take off your pants, put
    on some porn

Say good-bye to all your
    meanness,
Start getting busy with
    your penis;

It's likely best to
    gently stroke it,
But it's OK to tightly
    choke it;

Apply yourself with
    diligence,
And show the world
    you have good sense,

Soon you'll reach a
    joyful spasm:
No way to stop a good
    orgasm.

And then as stated,
    you'll explode,
Squirting out your
    studly load,

And pity as you
    then reflect
On all the others
    who neglect

Their manly member;
   what a shame,
No worse injustice
   can I name;

Then your Maker you will
   thank,
For giving us the
   the gift of wank.

—DFXP 7/11/23

Mistress Birthday-Girl

Julina my dear you're one
    of a kind,
You pleasure the body and
    also the mind,

Thus prompting me now
    on the date of your
    birth
To reflect on your gifts and
    exceptional worth,

You're lovely and sweet and
    adorable too,
And I always smile when
    thinking of you,

And so on this natal day
    greetings I send:
Have the happiest birth-
    day, My Beautiful
    Friend!

—DFXP 8/12/24

My Cock

My cock's a thing of
   great beauty,
'Cause always it does
   triple duty:
It lets me go pee,
Orgasms gives me,
And stands up when
   I see a cutie!

—DFXP 1/31/24

My Fav

I get all bothered
   and hot,
For a certain red-
   head's twat,
And while you may
   mock,
I prefer it to cock,
I'm real happy to eat
   what she's got!

—DFXP 2/22/24

My Fav 2

I love my fair red-
   headed maid,
And always I want
   to get laid,
But it is my cruel
   fate,
That I oft have to
   wait,
It takes me so long
   to get paid!

—DFXP 2/22/24

My Favorite Way

When I'm with some-
　　body on a date
My favorite way to
　　masturbate

Is spread my legs
　　with touching
　　feet,
My left hand rubs
　　my asshole—sweet!

And with my right I
　　stroke my cock,
Let fly the cum! Who
　　needs a sock!

The most important
　　thing I think,
Is to be held by girl
　　or twink,

Because I am no
　　brute or bum,
I need to feel love
　　when I cum!

—DFXP 12/12/23

My Friend

There is a woman whom
I know
Who picks me up when
I am low;

I think of her most
every day,
And gloom and sorrow
go away;

And though she really
has no fame,
My heart lifts when I
hear her name;

She's caring, smart and
very witty,
Plus I think she's very
pretty;

She loves to read; writes
poems too;
I'm privileged to receive
a few;

When at her best her
words evoke
Feelings to be read

or spoke

With eloquence and
brevity,
Whether grief or
levity;

She uses words to
advocate,
Protect the helpless
from the great,

And it is her natural
role
To comfort every
troubled soul;

What makes me happy
in the end
Is knowing that she is
my friend.

—DFXP 9/26/23

My Friend Sonja

Michael N. has manly pride
He's tough and surly too
But he's also got a female side
He'd like to show to you

He shaves and scrubs and scours
himself till all is smooth and clean,
And primps and preens for hours
on end; it's tough to be a queen

Mascara, lipstick and some rouge
And makeup do their thing
And lingerie's a subterfuge
That makes her body sing

For he's become a she my friend
This cannot be denied
A sexy chick by evening's end
Who walks the female side

She wears a brunette wig that's long
Hair's never in a mess
For evening wear she can't go wrong
In a black and slinky dress

Seduction of the macho types
Is now her goal and aim

She always lives up to the hype
And Sonja is her name.

—DFXP 6/10/23

Nut-Sack

In showing what I pack
I fear there is a lack—
You see that my dong
Is not very long,
But I do have a vein-y
nut sack!

—DFXP 9/7/24

Ode to Anorgasmia

When I was young,
A kind look could make
Me Squirt.
If you want that now,
You'll have to work.
Muscles tire and jaws ache,
You sweat and shake, and
You're quite happy to get
To the end of that date.

—DFXP Sept. 2023

Oldest Profession

They say an escort is
a call-girl;
I've met a number; each
was all-girl.
It's crass to call them
prostitutes,
Or whores or sluts of
less repute.

But if I must make
my confession,
To me they are a
bless'd profession.
None spread joy like
them you see.
Be safe! They also spread
VD.

—DFXP 5/17/23

On Sex

Sex, reduced to its basics
Is no more than a set of instinctive,
pleasurable physical behaviors;
Emotion, intellect, altruism and art
Are required to elevate it;
Without these additions, sex is
Two dogs copulating, that's all.

—DFXP 2/6/23

On Sexual Love

Sexual love's a hoot my sweet;
The positions are risqué;
Lovers might be on their feet,
Or switch'd round some other way.

Side-by-side is all the rage,
And so's tits o'er ass.
Does dignity increase with age?
Does gray hair bring on class?

The answer's No, if I'm to say;
I take on all positions;
Was traumatized the other day,
But now I'm in remission.

—DFXP 5/16/23

Only You

I've gay masseurs and
    escorts fair,
And two cross-dressers
    with great flair,
And many other such
    playmates,
For rompings out or
    evening dates;
I try so hard to please
    each one;
Until they're happy I'm
    not done;
But as I sit and
    ruminate
On possibly a sinner's
    fate,
There is one thing that
    may redeem,
My prospects and my
    self-esteem:
Your visage in my mind
    I see;
No other can compare to
    thee;
It's JUST with you I am
    in love
(So please give me no
    cliff-side shove!)

And don't think I don't
    give a shit:
For you all others
    I would quit.*

—DFXP 7/12/23

(*seriously, if you were
ever again mine, I would
be monogamous and faithful)

Our Titties

Our titties both
  yours and mine,
Have inspired this
  poetic line—
And ain't it too much
When we make nipples
  touch?
I can't think of nuthin'
  so fine!*

—DFXP 8/29/24

Oysters or Snails? (or, the Bisexual John's Dilemma)

I'm a poor connoisseur with
    limited cash,
And so again my choice
    I must rehash,

Against cruel fate my just
    outrage rails,
Which do I want, the
    oysters or snails?

In my heart I love oysters,
    a comforting treat,
But enjoyment I get out of
    snails: hard to beat.

Oysters soothe my
    emotions but snails
    are such fun,
I wish I were free to choose
    more than one;

Oysters are vaginas, worth
    my love and romance,
The snails are for play in a
    handsome guy's pants;

Which do I pick, it's so hard
    to choose,
If I could select both then
    I never would lose,

But I have no such
    freedom, and more
    is the pity,
The choice is a clear
    one: do I suck cock
    or titty?

—DFXP 11/11/23

Pen or Penis?

Taken in hand, with happy
Strokes, the seeds of
Generation begin to well up;
Self-exploration, solo creation,
Energetic attention, exhilarating
Motion, intrinsic energy
Striving for release; the
Explosion of desired expression,
The ecstasy of completion,
The unalloyed pleasure of self-
Realization; excitement followed by
The drowsy afterglow of bliss.

—DFXP 6/28/23

The Penis Poem

Sometimes think about
   a part
Of man's anatomy;
Its double function has
   its start
When exercised to pee.

Of course it's used for
   something more,
Much pleasanter employ-
   ment,
When stroked or sucked
   'til almost sore
For mutual enjoyment.

This stimulation of it
   makes
It stand so proud and
   pert,
And all the effort that it
   takes
Is worth it for the squirt.

The joy that this eruption
   brings
Is difficult to phrase:
The mind expands, the
   body sings;

It leaves you in a daze.

But lest you think it's
    all a lark,
Not worthy of more men-
    tion,
There is a side to this that's
    dark,
Requiring your attention.

With other people's cocks
    take care,
With caution choose the
    men:
You may be in for quite a
    scare,
Not knowing where they've
    been.

—DFXP 6/26/23

Perfect with a Pussy

Just 'cause sometimes
   I like cock,
I would never pussy
   mock,

And I'd never be so
   hasty,
Since, you know , it's
   pretty tasty,

And dicks are fun I
   can't deny,
But I love cunt, and
   here is why:

Cocks oft are stuck
   on hairy brutes
Who smell just like
   when my dog poots,

And though not always
   really ugly,
Sometimes they're just
   downright fuggly,

But twat you find on
   pretty girls,

With eyelashes and
    cutesy curls,

The girls are pretty,
    yes that's true,
Will smell way better
    than guys will do,

Each lady's like a
    graceful fairy,
And only head and
    muff are hairy,

Chicks are sweet and
    lovely too—
My favorite chick of
    all is you!

—DFXP 3/25/24

Polyamory Is Not a Dirty Word

I am Poly; I love.
Monos love too; they love
Just as hard and just as
Much as we do.
But if there is more than
One beloved, they are torn,
Distressed. They say to
Themselves, 'Which do I love?'
'There's no way out! How do I
Go on? (At least, those are the things I
Used to say to myself, in great Despair,
Before I was Poly.)
Or else they suppress it, fail to
Consciously acknowledge it, refuse to
Deal with it; in this way are neuroses
Born.
Polys are never torn.
We answer, 'So simple. Love both.
Love all.'
We say, 'How great is this? How happy am I?'
'How smiled upon are
The objects of my generous love?'
Monos think polyamory is a bad thing.
I wish they could understand how
Great a thing it is.

—DFXP 3/24/23

Pre-Sex Evacuation Too

> I'm finally ending my
>   slump,
> And soon it's your ass
>   that I'll hump,
> But when you fuck
>   mine,
> It better be fine,
> So first I must take
>   a big dump!

—DFXP 10/21/24

Pretty Clitty

Putting aside thoughts
    of tittie,
And all of the twat in
    this city,
The thing that I find
    the most pretty,
Is your sweet, adorable
    clitty.

Can't wait to plug in that
Hitachi 'Magic Wand'!

—DFXP 3/5/24

Pussy Power

Pussy power's
   notorious,
Twat is so damn
   glorious,

Behold the sight, lick
   pussy-juice,
The hairy slot and
   smell seduce,

But wait, there's
   more I have to
   say,
So you should
   strict attention
   pay,

And if you're hot to
   ask me why,
It's cause another
   hole's close by,

Anus, pussy
   aren't that far,
Shit-hole's next
   to the snack bar,

It seems a really
    nifty set-up
But penis-folk are
    always het up,

The guys aren't happy,
    want to shout,
That they try nine
    months to get out,

Live on in a cunt-
    starved spin,
Trying hard to get
    back in,

Well, let them stew
    and never fear,
Punani always will
    be dear,

You see it isn't just
    for guys:
Many gals have
    given sighs,

Lusting for their
    sister chick,
They like it so much
    more than dick,

Take your cue from
    Jodie Foster
If you think that cunt-
    love cost her,

Just listen up to what
    she says though,
She's a good and loyal
    Lesbo,

The guys just want to
    dip their wick,
Slurp their fill and
    wet their dick,

But they're all selfish
    hungry hogs,
Who should be treated
    like bad dogs,

So use your pussy
    every hour,
There's nothing like
    vagina-power!

—DFXP 4/2/24

Queer Fantasy

We sit side by side, reclining,
Sitting back into the piled-
Up pillows, with him on
My right, our nude bodies
Pressed together, legs
Spread, my right leg
Casually thrown over his
Left; our inside arms are
Crossed as well, and I
Hold and gently stroke
His erection with my right
Hand, gently masturbate
Myself with my left, with
Him helping with his right;
My bare ass feels so good
On the sheets, still clean
And dry, but not for long;
I spread my legs further,
Start thrusting my hips
With the masturbatory
Strokes, just a bit; feels
So good.
Our phalluses glisten,
Slick with coconut oil,
Helmets swollen and
Dark pink, the holes
Beginning to gape in
Anticipation of ecstatic

Ejaculation, pre-cum
Flowing freely, deliciously
Now.
We chat, joke, I turn my
Head to kiss his neck, his
Smoothly-shaved jawline;
No mouth-kissing! Do you
Think I'm some kind of fag?
We shift positions, with me
Putting my right arm behind
His his body, pulling him
Into me tighter, with him
Embracing me in return,
Both of us masturbating
In earnest now; pillows are
Thrown aside and we lie
Flat, with me on top, body-
To-body, bellies tightly
Together, arms around
Each other's necks, holding
Tightly, holding on holding
On and humping; now our
Cocks rub together, now I
Am fucking the delicious
Tight space made by our
Pressed-together bellies,
Even as he does the same;
I am feeling his big, hard
Hot cock against my
Cock, against my belly,

Thrusting back and forth,
Thrusting back and forth;
Too manly to smooch before,
We now lock lips, holding
The passionate kiss until
We are so far gone that
Our mouths just hang open,
Slack, tongues lolling, some-
Times touching; drooling;
The feeling is building rapid-
Ly now; we shiver; we
Groan; ohmygodohmygod
I'm cumming! We explode
As one, the semen squeezing
Out, mixing, spilling down
Onto the sheets, contraction
After contraction, wet pulse
After wet pulse as we gasp,
Moan: ohmygod! fuck! ohfuck!
Ecstasy! If I must die, let me
Die now, never more happily!
The sheets are wet, but the
Contractions soon mostly dry;
The feeling of intense orgasm
Lasts but a second or two
Longer then subsides into
Delicious contentment, I roll off
And collapse next to him as we
cross arms again, gently rub-
Bing each other's wet, messy

Belly, gently stroking each
Other's chubby but rapidly-
Softening, wet, messy cock;
Overcome now by queer
Affection, we kiss again.
I can be such a homo some-
Times!

—DFXP 12/7/23
(Pearl Harbor Day)

Queer Question

I love sex with people;
Some have vaginas and
Some have penises.
Am I straight? Am I queer?
Am I bi?
I love being a boy; I love
Everything about it.
I love my mustache, my
Boots and my shoes and
My boxer shorts. I love
My strength, the weights,
The iron, the gym. I love
Boxing and martial arts;
I have no talent, but love
These things anyway.
And I love girly things, lacy,
Frilly undies, garters, chokers,
Bustiers; I don't wish to wear
Them, but I want to fuck
Whoever is. And if that
Person is pretty and girly,
I don't care what's
Between their legs.
I'm happy to service vagina
Or penis; it pleasures me to
Pleasure either. But the penis
I love best is my own. And a
Nice ass is what it is. I'll take

Any nice one, but offer mine—
Nice indeed—to very few.
I have no guilt or shame
About my label, because I
Have no label. So if you
Know what I am, please
Tell me.

—DFXP 5/3/23

A Really Cool Observation

I was a late bloomer—I didn't start masturbating to completion until I was 16 years old. Since that time I would conservatively estimate that I have masturbated to orgasm at least once per week (probably more) every week for the last 44 years. That comes out to 2,288 self-induced ejaculations. At an average of 2.5 ml ejaculate volume per orgasm (Google/Wikipedia) that comes out to just about 6000 ml—or in other words 6 liters—or in other words about 1 and 1/2 GALLONS. A LOT of cum!

And I'm not bragging—I think this is about average: most guys my age could say the same.

The real studs are, like, 3-4 gallon guys! LOL –DFXP 1/30/23

Reflections

What do they call us?
What I am is not certain.
But they are nice.
But they are clean.
But they are careful.
We are pan; we are all.
We enjoy other
Genders, other sexualities,
Younger people,
Older people.
Beautiful people.
Fat, thin, dark, light.
Breasts, asses, legs,
Penises, clits, vulvas.
Soothing hands, soothing voices,
Kind faces, kind hearts.
Beautiful people.
They are beautiful to me,
I am beautiful to them.
We make each other happy.
We hurt no one.
At times flaunting and strutting,
But then needing to hide, yet
They still smile and have
Good wishes for the world.
I am different,
I am less,

I hate.
But I aspire to be like them.
The nicest people
Are poly sluts, queers, transgenders
Who would give you the shirts
Off their backs.
Their lives are insecure,
They are persecuted,
Spat upon.
They often hurt,
Sometimes die,
In forced isolation.
Why are they bad?
Why are they ostracized?
Why are they anathema?
Sometimes I think that
The world is upside-down.
And then I think that
It's better not to think.
They will make a difference but
I fear that I will not.

—DFXP 5/6/23

The Restless Mind

Whenever I am in the
    dumps,
requiring exits from
    my slumps,

I cast about and always
    find
that poetry soothes my
    restless mind;

I think that nothing can
    be sweeter
than childish rhyme and
    clumsy meter;

Love and sex and death
    and doom:
All yarn for my verbal
    loom;

And while to me it's
    satiating,
to others it's plain
    irritating;

Especially the way
    I text:
"What will this crazy

get to next?"

It's not my fault, oh
    can't you see?
It's just the way of
    those like me.

So please I ask you
    to be kind
to all like me with
    restless mind.

—DFXP 7/24/23

Rose

A secret I'll quickly
   disclose,
Is that I really like
   sucking toes,
And I'll be real
   blunt,
I love eating cunt,
But please serve it
   up with a rose.

—DFXP 5/13/24

Sacred Profanity

I've always pleasure in
  my sights,
Filled with am'rous
  appetites,

The ecstasy of flesh
  is great,
Emotions sated also
  rate;

When Cupid raises up
  his bow,
There's something else
  that you should know,

He makes my willy rise
  as well,
But there is also more to
  tell:

My mind and soul go all
  aquiver
(I even feel it in my
  liver)

A mighty urge possesses
  me
To versify my dear, you
  see,

It might be dirty, might
    be pure,
Might be weird or quite
    obscure,

Might sing the praises
    of a lass,
Or drool out lust for cocks
    and ass,

But whither goes my
    verbal art,
It springs eternal from
    my heart.

—DFXP 10/6/23

Self-Suck

I think of how I'd like
  to fuck,
More often now
  of how I'd suck

My own small dick
  if I just could,
And dreaming that
  my modest wood

Was 10-inch long
  or a whole foot,
The head right in
  my mouth I'd put

Then take that dong
  into my throat,
And suck like crazy
  while I'd gloat,

Because to suck
  myself you see
Is my greatest
  fantasy,

If I could give me
  oral pleasure,
That would be my

greatest treasure,

I'd swallow happy
    when I'd cum,
And put my load
    in my tum-tum,

When I'd be done
    I'd wear a grin,
Wipe semen-dribble
    from my chin,

Then look around and
    have pity,
For small-dicked guys
    who aren't me!

—DFXP 3/31/24

Sex Unlimited

With gender you can
   take your pick,
I'm up for any class;
I'll kiss your tits then
   suck your dick,
My thumb right up
your ass.

No need to file your-
   self away,
Or affix a sexist label,
Man or woman, straight
   or gay,
Or fluid and unstable.

As for myself I'm just a
   guy
With healthy sex
   desire;
You're into it; I don't
   ask why:
"Come on baby light
   my fire."*

What e'er you have
   between your thighs;
It's good by me my
   sweet;

I'll stroke you and draw
    forth your sighs,
And stimulate your
    meat.

And fuck your pussy
    guy or girl,
My thrusts will never
    stop,
'Til I've given you my
    jam of pearl.**
(I'm usually a 'top')

My words are clear,
    no meaning hid;
Need more? Here's
    just a few:
"We don't regret the
    things we did,
But the things we
    didn't do."

—DFXP 7/4/23

*With apologies to The Doors (1967)
**With thanks to Urban Dictionary

Sex Therapy

When the world just
　　gets me down,
Conspires to make my
　　smile a frown,

When anger and
　　anxiety
Are fueled by
　　notoriety

Of the evil men in
　　power
Who plot destruction
　　by the hour,

Just to stop the world
　　from turning
And set the whole
　　damn thing to burning,

What is it then that I
　　should do
To stop myself from
　　feeling blue?

I'll lick her pussy, take
　　her higher,
I'll suck his cock, my

pacifier,

I'll tongue an asshole,
      suck a tit,
That's the long and
      short of it,

And just to stop the
      pain and hurt,
I'll stroke my penis,
      make it squirt;

At the end of all this
      'sin' you see
That sex is my best
      therapy.

—DFXP 10/7/23

Shrimp-Cock

Red hot and feeling blue,
Don't quite know what to
    do:
My cock hangs limp
Like an old peeled
    shrimp,
And my balls stick
    together like glue.

—DFXP 8/12/24

Side

Lots of guys just like
   to fuck,
Me, I like to jerk and
   suck,

Stroke wet pussy,
   eat some poon,
Or wank and eat cum
   from a spoon,

Whether I'm with guy
   or girl,
To give my hand and
   tongue a whirl,

It cannot be too often
   stated:
Penetration's over-
   rated,

And although others
   may deride,
I'm so happy I'm a
   side.

—DFXP 7/11/24

Spiders in My Nose

True I got wrinkles, several
    warts, and kind of cruddy
    toes,
But what upsets my wife
    the most are spiders in
    my nose;

She saw some legs just
    dangling there,
Told me to cut my damn
    nose hair;

And I'm dismayed that
    she's assuming
It's a matter of my
    grooming;

And so I was at pains
    to say
That they weren't hairs,
    won't go away,

And if she could just
    listen please,
I'd tell of Belle and fair
    Louise:

Belle lives in my nostril

right,
She's brazen, always
    gives a fright,

Louise is in the left-
    hand nare,
She's bashful and
    would never scare;

They're boon compan-
    ions to my ears,
And take away their
    aural fears,

And if you should run
    out of sugar,
They're quick to lend
    a cup of booger;

They're there through
    thick and thin for me,
Can't ask for better
    company;

And so I tell my darling
    wife
I'll keep my spiders all
    my life!

—DFXP 3/28/24

Stink-Butt Cutie

I once met a
    beautiful lass,
Who had a severe
    itchy ass,
She complained,
"My hole's itching,
And it's not too
    bewitching,
But it's usually cured
    by my gas."

—DFXP 9/21/24

Stinky Finger

At night in bed I
  fantasize,
A vision comes before
  my eyes,

The image which
  before me passes
Is a parade of round
  smooth asses,

Could be those of
  guys or chicks:
Both give happiness
  to dicks,

My mind must go
  in that direction,
Which will produce
  a big erection,

And though I stay
  up way too late,
I always have to
  masturbate,

And just to make
  my pleasure keener,
I don't just stroke my

swollen wiener,

'Cause while I tug my
    man-meat pole,
I put a finger in my
    hole,

And feel cock pulse
    and anus pucker,
I'm such a dirty
    mother-fucker,

That probing finger's
    gonna stink,
That's really not so
    bad I think,

Because it gives me so
    much pleasure,
The orgasm is hard
    to measure,

I try for neatness but
    instead
Make semen messes
    in my bed,

And when I try to
    clean a bit,
My asshole finger

smells like shit,

I guess I'll have to
    wash my hand—
Oh no, it's on my
    wedding band!

Well that still
    is no big thing—
I can wash my
    marriage ring,

I so enjoy my anal
    kink,
That I don't mind
    a little stink.

—DFXP 4/2/24

Story About a New Friend

I recently made a new cross-dresser friend, "Sonja." We met online. I made arrangements to visit her at her house (in South Carolina, but less than an hour from Charlotte). I went there on Saturday week before last. I found the place no problem. She was very nice, everything went smoothly, we put each other at ease right away, and we did what we did. Afterwards we were lying back, relaxing, and she looked critically at me and said in all seriousness: "OK, so what's with the earrings?"

I laughed so hard I choked.

—DFXP 5/27/23

Tannhauser*

I wander lonely, as they
   say,
Searching ever and a
   day;

Driven on a endless
   quest
With very little time
   to rest;

Fearing that my soul
   will burn,
It's for bodies that I
   yearn;

And to see my needs
   are met,
I nightly prowl the
   internet.

Why is it I stay
   awake?
Perhaps the hormones
   that I take?

I fancy much of what
   I see;
Such sexual variety;

No shortage of new
   things to try
(And almost everyone
   is bi)

I could go on, but know
   I tend
To shock and sometimes
   to offend.

But there is never need
   to fear:
For I will never
   volunteer;

But should imagination
   fail,
Then I'll disclose in
   great detail;

And relate the things
   I must,
In explication of my
   lust.

I know I am a
   texting pest,
And should perhaps
   give it a rest;

And so dear lass give
    me this boon,
And don't give up on
    me too soon.

And grant to me a full
    exemption;
True love for you is my
    my redemption.

(*Sorry chick—you're
just going to have to
consult Wikipedia for
a synopsis.)

—DFXP 7/8/23

Tired

My sexual drive is
 hard-wired,
And my erotic spirit
 inspired,
Yet sometimes I'm
 limp
As an undercooked
 shrimp—
I guess my old dick
 is just tired.

—DFXP 7/7/24

To Mistress

Pain is just pleasure,
Domination submission,
To understand,
Assume the position.

Take it in the ass,
Or your cunt if you've
    got one,
To my kink mistress
    slut,
I ask: 'Ain't we got
    fun?'

—DFXP 2/23/24

Unwrapping the Present

When I arrive at your front door,
I inch it open, wanting more

I take you in my arms and then
It's Christmas morning once again

I crush you to me, kiss your mouth
And then my thoughts start drifting south

I feel like I'm a little tyke
With shiny toy or brand-new bike

As I unwrap my precious gift
It gives my spirit such a lift

Not just my spirit, I can tell
It gives my flesh a lift as well!

And that is why you'll always be
Much more than Santa Claus to me!

(You're waaaaay cuter—and anyway that beard is a turnoff!)

Merry Happy! LOL

—DFXP 9/6/23

Up Late
Jerking

I'm horny now, and
    it's so late,
But I don't want to
    masturbate,

I only have such
    apprehension
Because my penis
    needs attention,

My goal here isn't
    much contested—
It's to be sexually
    molested:

I want someone to
    stroke my cock,
To jerk me off into
    a sock,

To fondle me and
    then to suck,
But so far I am out
    of luck,

And while I wait, I
    know a trick:

To eat a pussy, suck
    a dick,

I really like 'em both
    the same—
I'm happy that my
    partners came,

And while I love a
    thorough jerking,
There is a discontent-
    ment lurking,

'Cause masturbation is
    no fun,
When it's just limited
    to one,

A lonely hobby
    to be sure,
And if I'm going to be
    impure,

I want SOMEONE to
    guide my hand,
And get me to the
    promised land.

—DFXP 2/26/24

The Vagueries of Love

If Destiny actually is
The power from above
Then it's a most unruly biz
The way it doles out love

Unlikeliest of lover pairs
Occasionally you see
And couple-ings both odd and rare
Appear most randomly

A prince is with his princess fair
And here's two handsome gents
Poor students who both deeply care
Their partner's Heaven-sent

And then there are non-binaries
And more exotic sorts
Two queens in glammed-up finery
Wise-cracking their retorts

Short chick is with a tall slim guy
Two black ladies are friends
It never pays to inquire why
All works out in the end

—DFXP 6/11/23

Wank Limerick

Some lovers enjoy the
   romance
Of a poem of love or
   slow dance,
But others save time
And get pleasure
   sublime
Just by putting their
   hand in their pants.

—DFXP 6/27/24

Wank-Mommy, Mistress of My Heart

A redhead of whom I'm
    quite fond
Is a fan of her Hitachi
    wand,
She enjoys several
    wanks,
Then my monkey she
    spanks,
And likes to see how
    I respond.

Happy Birthday!
You are a rare and
much-appreciated
joy in my life, as much
for your wits as for
your tits. I used to
have no interest in
you as a dominatrix,
but you have conquered
my heart— I will forever
be your loving sub.

Yours,

Daniel 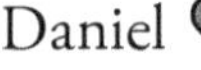  

Wank-Mommy

I'm with you butt-
    naked at leisure,
The joy in my dick
    hard to measure,
And nothing amiss,
As I snuggle and
    kiss,
Holding onto you during
    your pleasure.

—DFXP 8/9/24

What Could be Verse?

I've never been so upstanding,
    my detractors often mutter;
My delights are all frivolities,
    my behavior's in the gutter;

While I'm not plagued by dope
    or drugs or wicked reckless
    gambling,
There are many other avenues
    of sin down which I'm rambling;

There's gluttony and alcohol
    and sexual addictions,
Just to name a few of many
    less moral afflictions;

If you could all of these forgive,
    one thing you still would curse:
My penchant for abysmal rhyme
    and miserable verse.

—DFXP 11/11/23